CW00458274

Ali Baba and the Bunch

The Roycroft Dictiionary

Ali Baba and the Bunch

The Roycroft Dictiionary

1st Edition | ISBN: 978-3-75238-294-5

Place of Publication: Frankfurt am Main, Germany

Year of Publication: 2020

Outlook Verlag GmbH, Germany.

Reproduction of the original.

THE ROYCROFT DICTIONARY

by
Ali Baba and the Bunch

A DVERTISING: The education of the public as to who you are, where you are, and what you have to offer in way of skill, talent or commodity. The only man who should not advertise is the man who has nothing to offer the world in way of commodity or service.

ᴏ⟶

Aʙᴇʟ: The first squealer.

ᴏ⟶

Aʙʜᴏʀʀᴇɴᴄᴇ: 1. A pronounced feeling of dislike in the presence of what is superior or unattainable. 2. To discover one's real self and to slander somebody or something else in revenge. 3. A form of hate that suffers from *mal de mer*.

ᴏ⟶

Asʙᴇsᴛᴏs: 1. The white-hope of the damned. 2. A specially prepared paper upon which *The Philistine* is printed.

ᴏ⟶

Aʀsᴏɴ: To be careless in the use of fire. (General Sherman was at times more or less careless in the use of fire on his March to the Sea.—*Hon. Henry W. Grady.*)

ᴏ⟶

Aᴇʀᴏɴᴀᴜᴛ: A person who goes up in order to come down. Hence, a metaphysician.

ᴏ⟶

Aʙɴᴏʀᴍᴀʟ: To have intelligence, character or genius; to be less stupid than one's neighbor; to be better than the worst; to be one's self. *E. g.*, the writer of these lines.

ᴏ⟶

Aʙᴏᴅᴇ: 1. A place where one cleans one's teeth and occasionally sleeps. 2. A long counter with a gutter and a rail at the bottom over which one is served with any liquid in a glass. 3. Dwelling, fireside (obsolete in this sense). 4. A grave.

⚭

ABNEGATION: A plan for securing the thing in the easiest and surest way.

⚭

ACADEMIC: 1. Of, or pertaining to, fossils; vegetative; parasitic; the opposite of change, viable, evolution. 2. Relating to a society that promotes the love of the static and the immobile. 3. Apish, parrot-like, phonographic.

⚭

ADIEU: A prayer of thanksgiving uttered at parting.

⚭

ACQUAINTANCE: Any one we bow to politely at the opera or shake hands with warmly in a barroom, but whom we would kick out of our homes. Hence, any one who has refused us a loan.

⚭

ACT: 1. Thought in motion. 2. An actor who says he gets three thousand a week.

⚭

ABYSS: 1. The measureless gulf between literature and the American magazine. 2. The distance between a thinker and an editorial writer.

⚭

ARMY: A body of humanitarians that seeks to impress on another body of men the beauty of non-resistance, by exterminating them.

⚭

ABORIGINE: 1. A natural, unaffected person; one who has no conscience, who is honest, upright, and always at war. 2. A Deist, a Pantheist, who sees God in everything and feels His presence everywhere, even in his cannibalistic rites; hence, the first thinker in any country. 3. One who hates civilization and the *Ladies' Hum Journal*. 4. Any one who is mulcted, robbed, murdered, butchered, betrayed, in the name of progress.

⚭

ANARCHIST: 1. A Christian dilettante; one who casts a shadow on tomorrow while waiting for the Greek Kalends. 2. A mouther of sublime inanities. 3. One who maps and surveys the air and constructs dainty Utopias with the building-blocks quarried from his unbelievable credulity. 4. In the insane asylum of idealists, a man who imagines himself to be God. 5. A militant bourgeois who has deserted both Rome and Reason because he can not stand competition.

⚭

3

AMERICAN PLAN: A scheme for shortening human life through overeating.

◀━▶

ANANIAS: 1. The first ad-writer. 2. Any person who adapts the truth to his needs. 3. An ancient Saint George who slew the dragon Truth—hence, any popular hero or revealer who displays his grinders.

◀━▶

AGRICULTURIST: One who makes his money in town and blows it in the country.

◀━▶

ANGER: 1. A violent blushing and scampering up and down of the blood upon hearing the truth about ourselves; an epileptic condition produced by the presentation of a bill that is not yet due, just due, or overdue. A sudden tumescence of the ego and a furious exaltation of verbal powers upon losing a collar-button. 2. Before election, the righteous wrath of a candidate in the presence of evils that he has invented; after election-day, his wail in the presence of the grave he did not dig. *E. g.*, The devil (taking final leave of the Lord): "I am in anger with thee, Sire." The Lord: "For thee, son, 't will be a long time between heavens. So go to Hell and take thine Anger with thee."

◀━▶

ADMISSION: 1. To lie frankly and truthfully about something that can not possibly incriminate you. 2. To go into a place where one is not wanted; as, "A burglar gained admission to my house."

◀━▶

ADMIRATION: 1. The smile of Spite. 2. To secretly wish evil to one who has given us pleasure. 3. A form of shamefaced flattery. 4. To murder and go scot-free. *E. g.*, "I admire him very much." "Ah, so that is the reason he has become thoughtful!" From Bean's *Meditations of a Vegetarian*.

◀━▶

AFTERWARD: A space of time in which something happens after something else has happened, as, life, death; love, disillusion; riches, gout; wine, headache; unselfishness, regret.

◀━▶

ASSEMBLY: The Pantheon of the mediocre.

◀━▶

AUTOBIOGRAPHY: 1. Auto-intoxication. 2. Things which no one else will say about you, and which therefore you have to say of yourself.

◀━▶

APOSTLE: 1. A machine for recording a lie. 2. A person who has grown round-shouldered from following the spoor of another. 3. A lickspittle needed by philosophers in their business.

ALBANY: 1. A place beyond which Henry Hudson could not go. 2. The lobby of the White House. 3. Famous in history by the biennial meetings of the Blackmailers' Club. 4. Any place wherein a capitol is burned at a pre-established psychological moment. (There is a famous proverb which says, "Those who are in Albany escaped Sing Sing, and those who are in Sing Sing were on their way to Albany.")

ATHENS: See Pericles and Aspasia.

ART: 1. The vengeance of the Ideal on the Real. 2. Anything done by a man or a woman on paper, canvas, marble or a musical keyboard that people pretend to understand, and sometimes buy. 3. The antithesis of whatever becomes popular in the cultured world. 4. To cast out the dragons of virtue and hypocrisy by committing some imaginary sin and telling the world about it. 5. The beautiful way of doing things. 6. The expression of a man's joy in his work. 7. A matter of hair-cut and neckties. 8. The uplifting of the beautiful so that all may see and enjoy. 9. The utilization of love's exhaust. 10. Love's by-product.

ART-COLLECTOR: A man who operates a morgue for things rich, rare and precious.

ATHEIST: Any man who does not believe in himself.

ATHLETE MEX: Any man who throws the bull.

ATONEMENT: 1. Embolism of the will. 2. To raise a sin from a vice to a virtue. 3. A borax that kills the vermin of remorse, but that can not be relied upon to kibosh their breeding-place. 4. An immunity-bath in preparation for transgressions to come. (Among certain religious sects, the Day of Atonement is the day on which all gonofs line up for a fresh start.)

ATTENTION: Concentration of the mind on whatever will ultimately put something in the pocket; hence, in law and politics, the frame-up.

ACK: 1. That part of the body to which your friend directs his remarks when he tells you the truth. 2. A smooth surface composed of skin and bones which stretches between Land's End and John O'Groat's.

BAL-MASQUE: The coronation of Mephisto.

BALIVORAX: A Battle Creek Bellifiller, made from selected fidoes, fuddies, fresh freddies, chibots and chitterlings. Ladies love it, babies cry for it, and men who eat it are loved by the ladies who love it who have babies who cry for it. This is the filler fidgeted for by Juno before she weaned Hercules—who was no bottle-baby—and fed to him afterward. Ask your Bagpiper and take no other.

BEATITUDE: A rare and evanescent mental state caused by the reception of money that one has not earned. Synonyms: Windfall, remittance.

BEGGAR: A robber who has lost his nerve—a bandit with a streak of yellow in his ego.

BIDDLE: The act of introducing a prizefight in a Sunday School.

BILLYSUNDAY: 1. A theological jumping-jack, jerked by financial strings. 2. Any one with a pious emotional jag. 3. Hypnosis at so much per. 4. A person intent on saving his soul by religious rigmarole at the expense of reason. 5. To paddle away to Paradise in an orthodox canoe, and feel happy in the thought that most of the folks on the Big Ship are going to Hell.

BLOOMINGDALE: A condition of mind.

BASTARD: Any man who doubts his own immaculate conception.

BEAN: A dynamic spheroid, combustible under certain conditions.

BLABERINO: Any person who tells a person something a person says about him, which puts fishbones in the throat and brickbats in the Ostermoor of the person told.

BOOTY: 1. Whatever belongs to somebody that really belongs to somebody else, or whatever belongs to somebody else that really belongs to you or ought to belong to you if it did not belong to a third party—hence, anything at all. 2. Property in a transitional stage.

BAPTISM: Hydrocephalic abracadabra.

BARD: Anciently a poet; now a Poet-Laureate.

BOREDOM: 1. The essential nature of monogamy. 2. A period or rest between I Did and I Will. 3. A state of divine revelation wherein for a single moment we are carried by the giant of Eternal Inutility to the abysms and summits of the perpetual Nix. (The word *boredom* comes from Bore, a tired son of Noah. After the subsidence of the waters, Bore wandered about the earth, yawning and gaping and stretching, for at that time malaria oozed from many stagnant pools. Finally, absolutely exhausted, Bore, being afraid to be down on the damp and slimy soil, rested on the seventh day on his own bean, hence boredom.)

BUGHOUSE: 1. A condition of mind (See Boston) 2. The place where a person without funds is sent under certain conditions.

BUSINESS: Looking a payroll in the eye and kiting checks. 2. A method of reducing a landlady to her lowest terms.

BUSINESSMAN: One who gets the business and completes the transaction—all

7

the rest are clerks and laborers.

BUTLER: 1. A Person or Thing that has charge of the servants in a house belonging to another Person or Thing. 2. A tyrant without ears, eyes, organs, dimensions, passions.

BRAIN: A commodity as scarce as radium and more precious, used to fertilize ideas.

BOHEMIA: A good place in which to camp, but a very poor place in which to settle down.

BREAD: A foodstuff which the rich occasionally give to the poor as a substitute for cake.

ANNIBAL: 1. The conceiver and first practitioner of the eucharistic rite. 2. A place where a missionary may have a hell of a time. 3. A Pierrot whose pranks are side-splitting. 4. One who appreciates his fellow-being at his true worth. 5. The most subtle of living ironists. 6. Any one who takes his brother man at his physical valuation.

CARELESSNESS: 1. To have an eye on Eternity, wherein nothing matters. 2. To do a thing in the manner of a god who throws dice for the birth or death of a universe. 3. To perform an act wisely, but not too well.

8

COURTESY: 1. The court clothes of any two-legged predatory animal. 2. The oil that makes a juggernaut noiseless.

∝⊃

CHUMS: A condition of sophomorish propinquity that precedes a feud. (See furse and vendetta.) A state of chumminess between persons of opposite sex and suitable ages is more or less in the line of Nature. But that can't-get-along-without-you feeling between persons of the same sex is a form of hate and means that some third party is going to be beaned.

∝⊃

CIRCUMSTANCE: 1. The fresh banana-peel just around the corner. 2. *Ex-post-facto* knowledge of a series of incidents, episodes and laws which, had we known before doing something that we should not have done anyhow, we would have done otherwise, in the same way, or not at all. 3. The Shadowy Iago that follows us up and down life's promenades. 4. Man Friday to Chance.

∝⊃

CEREBELLUM: 1. The knapsack of Intelligence. 2. The *pons asinorum* between the mind and the cabeza. 3. A place whence, in democracies, politicians draw their strength, and in monarchies where the masses manufacture bombs and guillotines. *E. g.*, "Now suppose," began Professor Sapnoodle, "that a tiny elevator ran up the spine; we should then call the cerebellum the ceiling of the basement."

∝⊃

CHARITY: 1. A thing that begins at home, and usually stays there. 2. Bracing up Ralph Waldo Emerson's reputation by attributing to him literary mousetraps which he should have made, but didn't. (See Cheese.)

∝⊃

CHILDREN: Exquisite caskets of flesh that hold the scrolls of all our deeds.

∝⊃

CHAUFFEUR: The power behind the thrown.

∝⊃

CHEEK: 1. A drip-pan for tears. 2. Anciently, a part of the face; latterly, among women, the subsoil of rouge. 3. The principal asset of Ex-President Bombastes Furioso.

∝⊃

CHEF: The Messiah of gluttons; a Borgia of the scullery; one who crochets sweetbreads instead of cooking them.

∝⊃

CHALK: A deposit found at the top, bottom and middle and in the space between the bottom and middle and between the middle and top of American literature. (Chalk-line, used generally in the phrase, "to walk a chalk-line"; *E. g.*, the shortest way to reach the poor-house is to walk the chalk-line of probity).

CLIQUE: Friendship gone to seed.

COMMITTEE: A thing which takes a week to do what one good man can do in an hour.

CHRISTIAN: 1. One of a sect that despises and rejects the race from which its founder sprang. 2. A person who thinks he believes in a certain creed that he does not believe in, and thus is pied mentally, morally and arithmetically. 3. A man who keeps one day in the week holy and raises hell with folks and fauna the other six—sometimes.

CHURCH: A place where the Anointed of the Lord palm themselves off on one another. 2. A hall of echoes. 3. A counterpane for the dead. 4. An edifice wherein inspired fogyism gets its final degree.

CHICAGO TONGUE: A lengthening of the unruly member to a hammer-like proportion.

CONSCIENCE: 1. The muzzle of the will. 2. The Pecksniffian mask of the fundamental Bill Sykes. 3. The aspiration of Rosinante to be Pegasus.

CHURCH UNITY: Joining my church.

CIGARETTIST: One who is late every morning and fresh every evening.

CITY: 1. Any place where men have builded a jail, a bagnio, a gallows, a morgue, a church, a hospital, a saloon, and laid out a cemetery—hence a center of life. 2. A herding region; any part of the earth where ignorance and stupidity integrate, agglomerate and breed.

CIVILIZATION: A device for increasing human ills; a machine for the perpetuation of the weak; an ingenious contraption for spreading disease and hunger. (See war, harlot, politician, liar, Teddy, Sulzer, Murphy, hypocrisy, newspaper, forger, jail, policemen, lawyer, walking delegate, capitalist, poverty, clergyman.) *E. g.*, "Do you believe in civilization?" "Yep." From *The Confessions of Herr Krupp.*

⊂⊃

COMMONSENSE: The ability to detect values—to know a big thing from a little one. (I'd rather possess Commonsense than to have six degrees from Oxford. —*Fingy Conners' Confessions.*)

⊂⊃

CLOCK: 1. A telltale; a gossip; a blab. 2. A chink through which the Greta Secret leaks. 3. The Big Ben of eternity.

⊂⊃

COFFIN: 1. L'Envoi, the end of the legend. 2. An ornamental candy-box which no one cares to open. 3. A room without a door or a skylight.

⊂⊃

COLLEGE: A place where you have to go in order to find out that there is nothing in it. (See Marriage.)

⊂⊃

COLLEGE DEGREE: A social disgenic, as compared with proof of competence.

⊂⊃

COMIC: Tragedy viewed from the wings.

⊂⊃

COMPETITION: 1. The struggle for a cake of ice in hell. 2. The life of trade, and the death of the trader.

⊂⊃

CHIMERIC: To follow the right and get left. *E. g.*, A. He was chimeric. B. All the same, he went to the Chair like a man.

⊂⊃

CONCOCTION: 1. An imaginative mosaic distinguished from a lie in this, that a lie is "made up" and a concoction is "put together." 2. A social, religious, economic or political allegory, dogma, creed or program which lands some one in power and flattens out those who believe in it. 3. A mixture of dream and reality, sometimes called "Universe" or "World," put together by two strolling Super-Gentlemen Adventurers, sometimes known as God and Satan.

⊂⊃

CONFIDENCE: The one big lesson the world needs most to learn.

⊂⊃

CONSERVATIVE: One who is opposed to the things he is in favor of.

⊂⊃

COMPLIMENT: A sarcastic remark with a flavor of truth or not, as the case may be.

CONSOLE: To stab one in pain with the bare bodkin of pity.

CONTRADICTION: 1. Two lies disputing the roadway. 2. A head-on collision in which two trains of thought telescope each other.

COQUETRY: 1. An eye-shade worn by lubricity. 2. The colored glasses of The-Thing-Itself. 3. The death-tumbrel that Passion builds for its dreams.

CONSCIOUSNESS: A state wherein one becomes aware that he is being robbed, swindled or duped, by either a natural or an artificial law. Aside from his periods of sleep it may be said that man is always in a state of consciousness when voting, making love, or when succumbing to any other form of hypnotic suggestion.

CONVERSION: 1. To be suddenly seized by fright before a fiction or a fact. 2. To execute a mental and moral pirouette from one absurdity to a worse one. 3. To exhaust one pleasure and seek redemption in another. 4. A backslider from your own ideas to those of an inferior.

CO-OPERATION: Doing what I tell you to do, and doing it quick.

COURAGE: 1. A matter of the red corpuscle. 2. A matter of getting used to it. (It is oxygen that makes every attack, and without oxygen in his blood to back him, a man attacks nothing—not even a pie.—From Wilbur Nesbit's book *Bunc as I Have Found It.*)

CREED: A metaphor with ankylosis—a figure of speech frozen stiff with fright.

CURIOSITY: 1. A gulf that swallows gods, men, creeds, matter, worlds, philosophies. 2. A peephole in the brain through which one sees the pomp and ceremony of the Absurd. 3. A monstrous antenna that feels its way through matter and mind, and founders in the Infinite. 4. At its lowest, the instinct that boosts us up to peep over our neighbor's transom, symboled by a knot-hole.

CRITICS: Men who quarrel over the motive of a book that never had any.

CRIMINAL: One who does by illegal means what all the rest of us do legally.

CROMWELL (OLIVER): The father of Nell Gwynn.

CREDIT: The lifeblood of commerce.

CASTE: A Chinese Wall that deprives you of the society of sensible people.

CAIN: The first progressive.

AWN: 1. The beginning of a daily instalment in a serial story that will never end. 2. That mystical hour wherein Dives goes belching into dreamland and Lazarus comes out yawning carrying a dinner-pail.

DEATH: 1. To stop sinning suddenly. 2. To resign one's membership in the Ananias Club. 3. A readjustment of life's forces.

DEBT: 1. A rope to your foot, cockleburs in your hair, and a clothespin on your tongue. 2. The devil in disguise.

DEMAGOGUE: One whose highest ambition is to stand on the grave of a great dead industry and boast to an army of unemployed of his bloody deeds.

DECALOGUE: 1. The stakes that hold in its place the social circus-tent. 2. A collection of commandments formulated by a person who has broken them all. 3. An incubator in which eaglets are transformed into capons. 4. A fence that confines animals that can not climb or fly. (The most famous Decalogue is known as the Ten Commandments. Whoso has obeyed this Decalogue in toto has died obscure, poor, unsung, unwept, and overlooked by Clio.)

DOGMA: 1. A hard substance which forms in a soft brain; a coprolitic idea; a lie imperiously reiterated and authoritatively injected into the mind of one or more persons who believe they believe what some one else believes. 2. A paying thought or doctrine. 3. A recession into the Divine or Imperial—hence, the father of graft.

DEMOCRACY: 1. A form of government by popular ignorance. 2. The dwarf's paradise. 3. Any political system where male votes are substitutes for brains. (This word comes from the Abracadabra: "demo," lungs; "crazy," to rule; hence, to rule by caloric.)

DENNIS: The man who expresses the things he thinks other folks think he thinks.

DOLLAR: A disk of metal which has eucharistic qualities; a sacred, miraculous object, contact with which is looked upon as curative and prophylactic.

DIARY: 1. To see one's self as no one else cares to see us. 2. A book that describes the birth, effulgence and disappearance of pimples. 3. The lavatory of literature.

DIPLOMACY: An endeavor to side-step Nemesis.

DIPLOMAT: A man who says "perhaps" when he means no, as opposed to a woman who says "perhaps" when she means yes. (A man who says "no" is not a diplomat, and a woman who says "yes" is not a lady.)

DIGNITY: 1. A state of spiritual, mental or emotional starchiness that precedes a bluff. 2. A sartorial and tonsorial *chef-d'œuvre*. 3. The bodily attitude of a speaker or a preacher in the presence of people whose duty it is to believe he is not lying to them. 4. A mask we wear to hide our ignorance. (Man has dignity, woman has poise, animals have power; hence, dignity in a man or woman is anything that is a substitute for power.)

DISAPPOINTMENT: 1. The cradle of the ideal. 2. The skeleton of Purpose and the skull and crossbones of Desire. 3. A feeling in regard to the past that comes to every one on the Thirty-first of each December. 4. The final issue of any act begun yesterday, today or tomorrow. 5. The original road to Damascus and Horeb. 6. An alluvium deposited by the waves of Time in the human soul, and which becomes the basis of psychological Mont Blancs.

DISCORD: A guinea-hen, a peacock and a bluejay singing a trio.

DISADVANTAGE: Having too many advantages in life.

DEVIL: A god who has been bounced for conduct unbecoming a gentleman.

DOCTOR: 1. A person who has taken seriously the biblical injunction, "Physician, heel thyself!" 2. In Germany, a swashbuckler person with many scars, much admired by small boys and unhappily married ladies, and feared by shopkeepers.

DISINTERESTED: 1. Whatever is inconceivable. 2. A hypothetical ether that surrounds all forms of selfishness and naturalness. 3. That psychological interval when we look the other way before making a grab. 4. A monkey's mental attitude toward the hen.

DISHONORABLE: 1. To avoid infamy and almost attain respectability. 2. The first feeling we entertain toward each new acquaintance. 3. Any action whatsoever committed by a competitor.

DUTY: A pleasure which we try to make ourselves believe is a hardship.

DIVORCE: 1. A legal separation of two persons of the opposite sex who desire to respect and honor each other. 2. A marital derail.

DIVORCEE: 1. A female fugitive from injustice. 2. Any lady who is a Post-Graduate in Love's Correspondence-School.

DISCONTENT: 1. Inertia on a strike. 2. The mainspring of progress. 3. The starting-point in every man's career.

DISINHERIT: 1. The prankish action of the ghosts in cutting the pockets out of trousers. 2. To leave great sums of money to lawyers. 3. A method of insuring postmortem notoriety—and disappointment.

DOUBTER: 1. One who picks his teeth, blows his nose on his napkin, and yawns at the Lord's table. 2. A good-for-nothing who does not knock before entering the bathroom of the Faithful.

DREAM: 1. A place where the starving feel the pangs of gluttony, and the threadbare wear opera-hats and spats. 2. A magic mirror wherein the dead appear to mock us with their happiness. 3. A cerebral phenomenon caused on upper Fifth Avenue by eating too much, and on the lower East Side by eating too little. 4. The Valhalla and the Welsh Rabbit; the Brocken where the souls of the animals, fish and birds we have eaten hold their revels; a private theater where indigestion is the prompter.

DUCHESS: The feminine of Dutchman.

DYNAMO: Any man who has everything he eats, drinks, smokes and wears, charged.

EARTH 1. A small bean-shaped planet, full of noise, nonsense and noddies, created in order to swell the pockets of politicians. 2. A blister produced by the constant abrasion of motion against space.

EAT: 1. To prolong pain; to satisfy the anticipatory pleasure of hunger; to deliberately plan the contamination of the drinking-water of a people. 2. The demagogic demands of the belly. 3. A sinful or extravagant act among the destitute. 4. A sacred rite among the rich. 5. An artificial aid to conversation and the repetition of threadbare stories, generally off-color.

⚬⟷

EDUCATION: A form of self-delusion by those who muff every good wheeze.

⚬⟷

ECONOMICS: The science of the production, distribution and use of wealth, best understood by college professors on half-rations.

⚬⟷

EDITOR: 1. A person employed on a newspaper, whose business it is to separate the wheat from the chaff, and to see that the chaff is printed. 2. A delicate instrument for observing the development and flowering of the deadly mediocre and encouraging its growth. 3. A seraphic embryon; a smooth bore; a bit of sandpaper applied to all forms of originality by the publisher-proprietor; an emictory.

⚬⟷

ENEMY: 1. A counter-irritant of which you must get a few, or it's you for fatty degeneration of the cerebrum. 2. The friend who stings you into action. 3. Any one who tells the truth about you.

⚬⟷

EMPHASIS: To italicize a lie; to lay great stress on certain sounds that emanate from a larynx and that are intended to hypnotize a tympanum; to be impressive to the point of almost believing ourselves; the double chin of a declarative sentence; oratorical moth-balls.

⚬⟷

ENNUI: 1. The fourth dimension of action. 2. The looking-glass of the Infinite. 3. A state of time wherein seconds become days and hours become years. 4. A shop that contains nothing but a silent salesman, Death.

⚬⟷

EPIGRAM: 1. A vividly expressed truth that is so, or not, as the case may be. 2. A dash of wit and a jigger of wisdom, flavored with surprise.

⚬⟷

ENTHUSIASM: The great hill-climber.

⚬⟷

EQUITABLE: An ironical term meaning you can fool some of the people all the time.

⚬⟷

EQUITY: Simply a matter of the length of the judge's ears.

⊂⊃

EUCHARIST: Salvation by the pound, or by the pint. (If one should eat, say, a pound of eucharistic chips and drink two quarts of the holy water a day, one would be cleansed of all sin and be much richer in bacteria.)

⊂⊃

ETERNITY: 1. The Sunday of Time. 2. The sublimest thought of the brain of Ignorance. 3. A symphony written by a Beethoven of the ineffable x dimension. 4. The North Pole of the hours. 5. Monstrance of the Holy O. 6. A corrosive acid that obliterates Before and Afterward.

⊂⊃

EMANCIPATED MAN: One who has dared to think for himself, and thus has added to his list of enemies.

⊂⊃

EVOLUTION: 1. A word that has reclassified in an entertaining manner our impermeable and eternal ignorance. 2. The growth of a thing from the simple to the complex, and the wasting away of the complex until it is simpler than ever. 3. The one superstition that is cordially hated by theologues.

⊂⊃

EVERYBODY: 1. The square root of zero. 2. The leavings of individuality. 3. An agglomeration of bipeds who subsist on one another's shanks. 4. The Seventh Heaven of stupidity. 5. The cosmos of the pinhead. 6. Nobody in toto. 7. The collective and organized wisdom of the lowest forms of animal intelligence.

⊂⊃

EXPECTANCY: An exciting interval between rounds.

⊂⊃

EXPECTATION: 1. An optimistic feeling about an event that will never occur. 2. The secret of the persecution of the Jews, Christians and Mohammedans by one another. 3. The Goddess of Love. Synonyms: Tomorrow, next week, next year, next century, pretty soon—any imaginary space of time after the present moment.

⊂⊃

EXISTENCE: 1. A metaphysical term which originally meant joy, but which since the beginning of the Christian era has come to mean pain. 2. To be (used only in the phrase "to be damned"). 3. Merely to live, without eating or drinking. (In London, Paris and New York, this phenomenon is quite common.)

⊂⊃

EXPERIENCE: 1. The germ of power. 2. The name every one gives his mistakes. 3. Stinging and getting stung.

∞

EXPRESSION: 1. That mode of creation by which we coin things out of our hearts. (Nothing is of any value except that which you create for yourself, and no joy is joy save as it is the joy of self-expression.) 2. Mind speaking through its highest instrument, Man.

∞

EYE: 1. An organ of the human body which sees the universe as it is not, and transmits the same to the brain. 2. The soul's feelers and pickers.

∞

EYEBALL: 1. A small, miraculous globe that has the power to fabulize the external universe. 2. The spectacles of the brain; the peephole of consciousness.

∞

EPITAPH: 1. Postponed compliments. 2. Postmortem bull-con. 3. Qualifying for the Ananias Club.

∞

EUROPEAN: An inhabitant of New York City.

∞

EXECUTIVE: A man who can make quick decisions and is sometimes right.

ARMER: 1. A man who raises early feed for potato-bugs. 2. One who supplies raw stock for vaudeville jokes. 3. A man who makes his money in the country and blows it in when he comes to town. (Farms were first devised as an excuse for the Agricultural Department at Washington.)

FAILURE: 1. The man who can tell others what to do and how to do it, but never does it himself. 2. A man who has blundered, but is not able to cash in the experience.

FASHION: A barricade behind which men hide their nothingness.

FAME: To have your name paged by the "buttons" of a fashionable hotel.

FAITH: 1. The effort to believe that which your commonsense tells you is not true. 2. The first requisite in success.

FAKE: An event that occurs every four years in the United States; hence, by extension, anything popular.

FAMILY LINE: The clothes-line.

FAST TRAIN: One that has no diner.

FEAR: 1. A club used by priests, presidents, kings and policemen to keep the people from recovering stolen goods. 2. The thought of admitted inferiority. 3. The rock on which we split.

FEATHERS: Secondary sex advertisements made of fiber and horsetails, and used on ladies' lids as eye-gougers and such.

FEUD: A fool idea fanned into flame by a fool friend.

FEMINIST MOVEMENT: 1. A hot desire to step on the male tumble-bug. 2. An uneasy, eccentric, patho-psychio gyration, caused by disappointment or thwarted ambition. 3. A loose cam or a cosmic monkeywrench in the convolutions.

FIFTH AVENUE: 1. The widow's chance. 2. A rabbit-warren. 3. The underworld of the upper world. (Fifth Avenue begins at the Washington Arch and really ends at Fifty-ninth Street. Above Fifty-ninth Street one goes into the sacred precincts of monasteries and nunneries. In this district the inhabitants are divided into two classes: those who barely live and those who live barely.)

Fly: A sententious, epigrammatic stylist who puts a period after each utterance.

Folderol: Talk or conversation of any kind between a man and a woman that does not contain an invitation or a promise.

Forbearance: 1. To forgive an enemy who has been shorn of power. 2. To buy golden opinions of one's self. 3. To slay with irony or pity.

Forecast: To observe that which has passed, and guess it will happen again; to anticipate the future by guessing at the past; to predict that an event will happen, if it does, by basing calculations on events that have already happened, if they did. (One may forecast and be right, wrong, or neither. It depends.)

First Requisites: 1. Belief in yourself. 2. Pride in your work. 3. Useful hands, clear eyes, and a good breath.

Forehead: 1. The facade of a cosmic bagnio. 2. A screen that hides the obscene. 3. The ramparts of a portable Bastile.

Fortitude: That quality of mind which does not care what happens so long as it does not happen to us.

Forum: A safety-valve for letting out superfluous air. *E. g.,* "Let the Forum always be open to the people, and let the treasury always be open to us."— From Titus Livy's *Psychology of the First Contractor.*

Fra: A literary silo that feeds the world.

Frame-Up: See Brandeisism in the last edition of the *Century Dictionary.*

Friendship: 1. Something that by any other name would be as brittle. 2. A tacit agreement between two enemies to work together for common swag. 3. The aspiration to boredom. 4. To do unto some one that which you would not allow him to do unto you.

Friend: The masterpiece of Nature.

FRAT: 1. A scheme whereby you lock the world out by shutting yourself in. 2. A non-productive plan of self-incarceration in a brain bastile by a mental midge of either sex, or none. 3. A make-believe compact for purposes of piffle. (See snip-pity, top-lofty, tabascoish, supercilious.)

AIETY: 1. An effervescence of spirits produced by the expectation or the receipt of money. 2. The emotion of a poor person on learning of the death of a rich relative.

━○━

GALLANT: 1. To remember one is a gentleman in spite of one's birth and training. 2. To give up your seat in a car to a woman, and tread on your neighbor's foot to get even. 3. To do a perfectly unselfish act from selfish motives.

━○━

GENT: A chauffeur who has a cab-driver for a chum.

━○━

GENTLEMAN: One who is gentle toward the friendless.

━○━

GLORY: The five senses of the dead.

━○━

GENIUS: 1. One who offends his time, his country and his relatives; hence, any person whose birthday is celebrated throughout the world about one hundred years after he has been crucified, burned, ostracized or otherwise put to death. 2. One who stands at both ends of a perspective; simultaneity of sight; to be one's self plus; to be synonym and antonym to everything. 3. The ability to act wisely without precedent—the power to do the right thing for the first time. 4. A capacity for evading hard work.

GIVETH: The lisping tense of give. *E. g.*, "He giveth His beloved sleep."— From *The Ironic Sayings of Jehovah*.

GOSSIP: 1. Vice enjoyed vicariously—the sweet, subtle satisfaction without the risk. 2. The lack of a worthy theme.

GLUTTON: A poor man who eats too much, as contradistinguished from a gourmand, who is a rich man who "lives well."

GOD: 1. The John Doe of philosophy and religion. 2. The first atheist. 3. A puzzle-editor.

GOD AND SATAN: The Pathe Freres of existence.

GODDESS: A Super-Huzzy mated with an apotheosized Super-Thug.

GOOD HABITS: Mentors and servants that regulate your sleep, your work and your thought.

GOOD SPORT: A man whose soul is equipped with automatic lubrication.

GOOD LUCK: Tenacity of purpose.

GOVERNMENT: A kind of legalized pillage.

GOURMAND: A rich man who eats the surplus production of the world's foodstuffs that the starving are too niggardly to purchase.

GRAMMAR: The grave of letters.

GRAFT: An agrarian expression first used by Ali Baba.

GUESSWORK: A shallow depression, pit, or cavity in the consciousness of an editorial writer when he is warning the people.

GREAT MAN: One who perceives the unseen, and knows the obvious.

GUTTER: The Lourdes of the puritanical mind, where it finds what it seeks.

GROUCHERINO: One whose life is just one dam kick after another.

GRATITUDE: A lively sense of anticipation concerning favors about to be received.

GUMMA: A substance that forms in the cabeza by an overindulgence in mint juleps; hence, to become a Super-Brute or a political Has-Been.

GRIEF: 1. The telescope of the emotions that unfolds to your eye the meaning of all worlds. 2. The overtones in all joy. 3. The pleasure that lasts the longest. 4. The tears of Memory. 5. The vice of weakness and the virtue of strength.

APPINESS: 1. Something that might have happened yesterday, but which will never happen tomorrow. 2. A postprandial state of mind, which is most often a presage of acute gastritis. 3. A loving-cup, the bottom of which is like a sieve. 4. A mental state compounded of wine, women and tobacco. 5. The exploitation and final triumph of an instinct in the individual that society has branded as wicked or dangerous. 6. Forgetting self in useful effort. 7. A habit—cultivate it.

HABIT: The buffer of our feelings; the armor that protects our nerve-force; the great economizer of energy.

⊂⊃

HEART: An organ in the human body whence comes the impulse to get divorced.

⊂⊃

HAGGIS: The quintessence of all that has been said by all the Presidents, Governors, and Mayors in the United States since Eighteen Hundred Eighty-nine.

⊂⊃

HAND: 1. A conventionalized bread-hook. 2. An attachment at the end of the human arm which gives to another a lemon, or something that the owner of the arm can no longer use or that is harmful to him.

⊂⊃

HAIR: The Olympus of the pediculidæ.

⊂⊃

HEAVEN: 1. The Coney Island of the Christian imagination. 2. Largely a matter of digestion. 3. An orphan asylum where institutionalism reigns. 4. A penitential colony where the virtuous and the good are condemned to eternal fellowship for their stupidities uttered on earth.

⊂⊃

HATE: 1. The shoal on which our bark is stranded. 2. A habit.

⊂⊃

HAS-BEEN: Any man who thinks he has arrived.

⊂⊃

HELL: 1. A Papal bull. 2. An extinct volcano. 3. The Pantheon of the brave. 4. An ancient conflagration that was checked when Voltaire invented the asbestos intellect. 5. A theological corn, wart or tumor. 6. The sense of separateness. 7. Three telephone systems in a town. 8. An invitation to go sightseeing. *E. g.,* "If I'd only had a parachute at the time I would have gone to hell gracefully and taken a record for descent."—From Lucifer's *Confessions of a Ticket-o'-Leave Man.*

⊂⊃

HUSBAND: A booby prize in life's lottery.

⊂⊃

HELTA-SKELTA: The new substitute for Strenuosity. Puts you to sleep while you work. Helta-Skelta is a prepossessing product made from posthole polyglot piecrust, and is warranted free from teddine, swaboda, korona, kabo and karezza. Served face to face with cream or without, it is spit out as soon as chewed, and can not be swallowed. Locate the lavatory and try a free sample.

◁▷

HEN: The only animal in Nature that can lay around and make money.

◁▷

HIGHBROW: 1. A person who has grown so wise that the obvious escapes him. 2. One who reveres knowledge with superstitious awe, and whose worship of observation approaches the ecstatic. 3. One who believes that an atom is a monstrance that conceals the Holy Ghost of Force.

◁▷

HIGHFLYER: Any man who rides on the running-board, when he might just as well be inside the limousine.

◁▷

HISTORY: 1. A collection of epitaphs. 2. Gossip well told.

◁▷

HOME: 1. A place where we go to change our clothes so as to go somewhere else. 2. The abode of the heart

◁▷

HUMOR: The tabasco sauce that gives life a flavor.

◁▷

HUMILITY: 1. The slippered patience of the disinherited. 2. The grogginess of the Ego. 3. To recede to the very bottom of one's own littleness. 4. The Marseillaise of the disappointed. 5. The odor of sanctity. 6. An Iago in plush and lavender. 7. Pride getting ready for a Pounce.

◁▷

HONEYMOON: 1. A happiness not quite worn out. 2. A postlude to a wedding-march and a prelude to a funeral ditto. *E. g.*, "I did not drive Adam and Eve out of Eden because they ate my pet pippin, but because they insisted on carrying on their honeymoon before the modest animals."—From *The Private Journal of Démiurge*.

◁▷

HOPE: 1. A substitute for yesterday. 2. A mask that dying persons wear. 3. A system of metaphysics founded by Ananias. Antonyms: Reason, imagination, experience.

◁▷

HOUSE: 1. A building with four walls and a roof. 2. A rendezvous for burglars. 3. A dormitory for servants. 4. The Mecca of bedbugs. (The difference between a house and a home is this: A house may fall down, but a home is broken up.)

HUMAN LOVE: The one indestructible thing in Nature.

HUMAN DYNAMO: Any man who gets everything charged.

DEAL: 1. The dreams of a sin to come. 2. The mirage of failure. 3. The venom of the lost. 4. An excuse for murder, tyranny or for self-aggrandizement. 5. Any theory that justifies our secret itch.

IDEALIST: 1. A glassblower. 2. A somnambulist who insists on stepping out of a solid window into the air. 3. A person who lives in a tower of porcelain and dines on pumpernickel and lobscouse. 4. A man who fills his gasoline-tank with attar of roses and expects the motor to run.

INTELLIGENCE: The grand inquisitor that tortures from every truth the confession that it lies, and from every lie a confession of its divine necessity.

IDEAL LIFE: Man's normal life, as we shall some day know it.

IF: 1. A tightrope that stretches from But to But. 2. A small, magical, automatic hinge that can swing the doors of Chance in any direction. 3. A fatality endowed with free will. 4. The verbal sword of Damocles. 5. A dizzy precipice at the end of every declarative sentence. 6. A pole around which the future and the past play hide-and-seek. 7. The vorspiel to the piker's threnody. *E. g.* (Scene: a narrow bridge.): "Let me pass, fellow! my name is Must, and I desire to cross." If (standing in the middle of the bridge): "You damn fool, don't you see I am the end of the bridge? There is no Must nor Might that can go beyond me."

∝

IMITATION: The sincerest form of insult.

∝

IGNORAMUS: Any man who flatters himself that he is educated.

∝

IMAGINATION: 1. A marvelous little multicolored drugget that covers the rough and splintered floor of reality. 2. A haunted chateau. 3. A vestibule between Time and Eternity. 4. The giant enemy of reality. 5. The red Pantheon of Lucifer. 6. The candle-gleam of science; the flambeau of the lover; the constellated nebulæ of the poet. 7. The glittering west-dust of a hidden innominate sun. 8. The seigniory of untrammeled instincts; the fief of unsanctified dreams; the palfrey that carries us toward nebulous spiritual hills. 9. The plasma of gods. 10. Puck strapped to the back of Balaam's ass. 11. The Shakespeare of mental faculties. 12. The avatar of the emotions. 13. A golden key that unlocks the bastile of logic. 14. A ladder to the fourth dimension. 15. A sublime liar. 16. Taking the halter off your thoughts and giving them a good kick behind. 17. Sympathy illumined by brains.

∝

IMITATOR: A man who succeeds in being an imitation.

∝

IMMORTALITY: 1. A reward given to infidels and atheists by a somewhat humorous God, for not groveling before Him and annoying Him with importunities. 2. A system of punishment for suicides, which makes suicide impossible, thereby putting one over on the ingrate who was tired of the gift of life, by compelling him to live forever, willy-nilly. 3. A valueless thing, because unlimited in quantity, which those hotly intent upon achieving will forfeit through the law which provides that that for which we clutch we lose. 4. A condition sought by political officeholders where the incumbent never either dies or resigns. 5. A state of being encouraged by annuitants, and those who live in the Garden of Allah-Money. 6. A flimflam offer by a theologian of inchoate title to improved real estate in the Sky for real estate, rentals and cash on Earth. 7. A doctrine that the rich teach the poor for good and sufficient reasons. 8. Divine Compensation for the starving. 9. A superfluous addition to life; to go on living after one desires and hopes to remain dead.

∝

INDEPENDENCE: An achievement, not a bequest.

∝

IMPERIALISM: Tyranny, hiding behind the sacred name of Humanity.

INFIDEL: One who defames his Creator and impeaches his own reason by believing in Orthodox Christianity.

INFIDELITY: To remain faithful to one's self, and to be unfaithful to some one else's faith. In religion, to think; in the marriage institution, to fall in love; in business, to do the thing to the other fellow that the other fellow intends to do to you, and do it first.

ISSUE: In physiology, something that comes up and out; in politics, something that goes down and in.

INGRATITUDE: 1. A girl who is too busy to acknowledge receipt of a Christmas present. 2. The portion of the man who has done well; and a fight with the fox you have warmed into life is imminent.

INFUSORIA: The entire human race with the exception of Homer, Richard Wagner, Dante, Victor Hugo, Balzac, Rodin, Raphael, Æschylus, Shakespeare, Schopenhauer and Edward Bok, in whose tremendous skulls we live and move and have our being, like a whirlwind of germs in the vats of the Absolute.

INGRATE: Any person who has got something for nothing, and wants more on the same terms.

INITIATIVE: Doing the right thing without being told.

IRONY: The cactus-plant that sprouts over the tomb of our dead illusions.

UDICIOUS: 1. A state of mind wherein things are weighed in an imponderable scale; a conjunction of two negatives in a void. 2. To be wanting in foolishness, character or brains. 3. An exquisite and delicate perception of the difference between two things that are exactly alike, or the total unlikeness between two things that are absolutely different. 4. An umbrella to be carried on clear days as well as on rainy ones, thus protecting the possessor from everything. 5. To lie flat on your puss while the juggernaut of Opinion goes over you; to stand perfectly still between two streetcars going in opposite directions. 6. To see what's coming and avoid it by taking all sides.

JOURNALIST: A newspaperman out of a job.

JURY: 1. The stupidity of one brain multiplied by twelve. 2. A collection of sedentary owls. 3. The humble apology of Civilization to Savagery. *E. g.*, "Whatever exists may be touched, but a jury is an exception to this universal law—it must be reached."

JUSTICE: A system of revenge where the State imitates the criminal.

JOHN DOUGH PROCEEDINGS: A hunt for graftheimers.

JUDGE: 1. A man with ankylosis of the ego, who is jealous of the stenographer for sufficient reasons. 2. One who learns law from lawyers and is excluded from the game, getting his in honors.

ING: 1. In the presence of genius, a pleb. 2. A vestige. 3. One whose chief diversion lately has been to watch himself grow beautifully less. 4. A First Cause run to seed. 5. Divine Right tempered by bombs.

—

KINDERGARTEN: The greatest scheme ever devised—for the education of parents.

—

KNOCKING: A slow but sure way of putting the skids under your prospects. Push in the door softly, and all things are yours—knock and nothing shall be opened unto you.

—

KNOWLEDGE: The distilled essence of our intuitions, corroborated by experience. Knowledge is what I know; wisdom is what I see; theology is what I guess.

ATER: The Utopia of Postponement; a marvelous door of gold at the end of every perspective, to which Procrastination holds the keys.

The Concierge of tomorrow. (Some things are done sooner, others are done now, but most things are done later; hence, manana, dreams and regrets.)

⊂⊃

LAUGHTER: 1. The sound you always hear when you chase your hat down the street. 2. Nature's rest-cure for tired nerves. 3. The solace of the sad. 4. A facial sunburst that is fatal to the glooms.

⊂⊃

LAW: 1. A scheme for protecting the parasite and prolonging the life of the rogue, averting the natural consequences which would otherwise come to them. 2. The crystallization of public opinion.

⊂⊃

LAWYER: 1. A person who takes this from that, with the result that That hath not where to lay his head. 2. An unnecessary evil. 3. The only man in whom ignorance of the law is not punished.

⊂⊃

LEARN: To add to one's ignorance by extending the knowledge we have of the things that we can never know.

⊂⊃

LIE: The weapon of defense that kind Providence provides for the protection of the oppressed.

⊂⊃

LEVITATION: The creeping up of your trousers when you ride horseback, so that they supply you a necktie.

⊂⊃

LANGUAGE: The tool of the mind.

⊂⊃

LIBELOUS: To be tactless in type.

⊂⊃

LIAR: 1. One who tells the truth about something that never happened; hence, a poet, a preacher, a politician, or an Arctic explorer. 2. An expert witness on the side of the Prosecution, or any witness called by the Defense. 3. One who reasons far ahead of his time; a seer. (As all combinations of facts must occur in endless time, the liar, no matter how absurd his statement, is uttering a truth, because he is stating a fact that has occurred or will occur at some future date. Thus, a liar, in the sense of one who utters a falsehood, can not be said, strictly speaking, to exist. As dirt is merely nectar in the process of evolving, so a liar is an observer born out of his time. He is the victim of a divine prank.)

⊂⊃

Literature: The art of saying a thing by saying something else just as good.

Liberty: 1. A password in universal use, and hence of no value. 2. The slogan of a party or sect that seeks to enslave some other party or sect. 3. The lost latchkey to the Citadel of Power. 4. The sacred aeroplane of King Ego. 5. The right to go forth unimpeded from any place, and also to come back. 6. The Northwest Passage to Nowhere. 7. The thing Patrick Henry asked for when the bartender asked him what he would have. 8. Only a comparative term. 9. Responsibility—that is why most men dread it.

Library: A place where the dead lie.

Logic: An instrument used for bolstering a prejudice.

Loafer: The man who is usually busy keeping some one else from working.

Life: 1. An ante-mortem statement; the intrigue of force and matter; the insomnia of death; a log-jam on the stream of life. 2. The pursuit of the superfluous. 3. The cupola of a tomb. 4. A game something like Blind Man's Buff. 5. The paradise of liars. 6. A compromise between Fate and Freewill. 7. A warfare between the sexes. 8. What you choose to make it. 9. A bank-account with so much divine energy at your disposal. 10. Just one improper number after another. 11. The interval between the time your teeth are almost through and you are almost through with your teeth. 12. An affirmative between two negatives.

Lonely: A peculiar feeling caused by the presence of one or more bores.

Lovers: Unconscious comedians.

Love: The third rail for Life's Empire State Express. The beginning of all wisdom, all sympathy, all compassion, all art, all religion.

Living: A mode of wasting time from the cradle to the grave consecrated by immemorial usage.

Litigation: A form of hell whereby money is transferred from the pockets of the proletariat to that of lawyers.

ANKIND: 1. A nomadic savage that has wandered over the face of the earth from East to West in order to reach the East so it could go West again. It has left many traces of its life—barrooms, brothels, jails, churches, gallows, best sellers, etc. 2. In the animal kingdom, a surreptitious and supposititious supererogation. 3. Among the Simians a place equivalent to our hell. "Oh, you go to Mankind," is quite frequently heard in the African jungle, even in the best society.

MAHIN: A jumbo of publicity who puts it over.

MENTAL DISSOLUTION: That condition where you are perfectly satisfied with your religion, education and government.

MAN: 1. A super-simian. 2. Holy dicebox of the devil. 3. God's scrapbook. 4. Anything allowed to stand at a public bar. 5. A biped with feathers in his or her hat. 6. A being said to be the highest work of God—and who admits it. 7. Any creature that creates a Creator in his own image. 8. A god in the crib.

MAN-HATER: A woman who, finding herself no longer acceptable to man, flirts with Mephisto.

MARRIAGE: 1. A legal or religious ceremony by which two persons of the opposite sex solemnly agree to harass and spy on each other for ninety-nine years, or until death do them join. 2. A way-station, not the end of the journey.

3. The aspiration of two vowels to be a diphthong. 4. Love's demitasse.

⊂⊃

MAYOR: 1. *Particeps criminis.* 2. The head and front of our offending. 3. Polonius Pecksniff, who plays Bottom for a stipend. 4. A chaste, honorable, virtuous person whose private life is made inviolable by the libel laws. 5. A prickly sensation in the back of Folly and Revelry. 6. The culmination, zenith, equator and pediment of self-sufficient mediocrity. 7. A crow's-nest from which one may see the perpetually receding horizons of the Governorship and the Presidency. 8. A chef of morality. 9. Any person afflicted with primary, secondary or tertiary holiness. 10. A palm-reader. 11. A nebulous cluster of thought-embryons resolved into a gaseous state. 12. The nosebag of public decency. 13. The *alter ego* of organized cant. 14. The critic of impure reason. 15. Lobster emeritus. 16. A person who takes an oath to love, honor and obey Tartuffe.

⊂⊃

MANHOLES: The apertures in a peekaboo shirtwaist.

⊂⊃

MARTYR: Any man who is willing to sacrifice others for his "cause."

⊂⊃

MASTER-MAN: A man who is master of one person—himself.

⊂⊃

MASTERSHIP: Industry, concentration, self-confidence.

⊂⊃

MATHEMATICS: A tentative agreement that two and two make four.

⊂⊃

MATTEAWAN: The antechamber of liberty for a murder-gent.

⊂⊃

MILITARISM: A fever for conquest, with Peace for a shield, using music and brass buttons to dazzle and divert the Populace.

⊂⊃

MERCY: 1. The charity of tyrants. 2. The forgiveness of one scoundrel by another. 3. The culmination of the Will-to-Power and its final apotheosis. 4. A quality which, like soup, the more it is strained the less soup and the more water you have. 5. In war a universal mode of subjugating a people.

MEPHISTO: The fourth person in the Holy Trinity.

MILITANCY: A fixed, fighting mental attitude that will never know when the war is over.

MIDNIGHT: 1. The Pole of the hours; a pincushion on which sparkle all the seconds of a day; the keel of the good ship Tomorrow. 2. A chimney whence the dreams of today issue in smoke.

METAPHYSICS: 1. An attempt to define a thing and by so doing escape the bother of understanding it. 2. The explanation of a thing by a person who does not understand it.

MIDDLEMAN: One who works both ends against the middle.

MILLENNIUM: 1. A thousand years beginning with Now and ending with Then. 2. A mythical period when every one will pay his debts and begin tomorrow again on renewed credit. 3. A religious cycle which has no visible means of support, even admitting the ideality of time. Hence, by extension and usage— [Here insert a Mergenthaler pi line of thirty-two ems.]

MAMMON: The Pope of Protestantism.

MUCKRAKER: One who sits on the fence and defames American enterprise as it marches by.

MIRACLE: 1. A happening seen by four men at once, but by no one man in particular—hence, a collective, but otherwise untrue, fact. 2. The minutiæ of cosmologies. 3. A physical event described by those to whom it was related by men who did not see it. 4. A portent that precedes the coming of a Liar with letters patent from Nowhere, or a series of extraordinary occurrences that attend his comings and goings and mouthings that in no way equal in majesty, beauty or mystery the simplest commonplace of his life. (No god, demigod, or other parasite of human ignorance is complete without miracles, for it is only the natural and commonplace that are unbelievable.)

MOTHERHOOD: The headliner in God's great vaudeville.

MISSIONARIES: Sincere, self-deceived persons suffering from meddler's itch.

MISTRESS: 1. A female who has rights, as distinguished from a married woman, who has duties. 2. One whose respect and love some married men may hold without the non-transferable license in the bottom of a trunk.

MARTYRDOM: The sweet apotheosis of the things we do not care to avoid.

MINUTE: 1. The crutch on which the Hour leans as it limps into Eternity. 2. A space of time in which we dream of something that will never come true, or form a resolution that another minute effaces.

MODESTY: 1. A beau-catcher that young ladies wear and women affect. 2. In a sweetmeat, the souffle through which we dig to reach the plums. 3. The blush on the face of Desire at the consciousness of its own immodesty. 4. Among men modesty is the will-to-wait and seize. 5. Venom, who sidles into corners and shuns the limelight, so that he may the better see. 6. The attitude of mind that precedes the pounce. 7. The subtlest symptom of paranoia. 8. Egotism turned wrong side out.

MUMMY: 1. An unobjectionable party whose motives are not questioned. 2. One who is not in business for his health. 3. Any one who does not advertise.

MORALITY: 1. The formaldehyde of theology. 2. The line of conduct that pays.

MORALIST: 1. A beautified eunuch. 2. One self-elected to make the stupid more stupid. 3. Any one skilled in the science of pornography. 4. A retired roue. 5. One of the Sacred Legion of Coprolitis.

MORGUE: The pantheon of the unremembered; Death's shop-window.

MUNSEY: 1. Any publisher who does much business on small mental capital. 2. *Verb*: To munsey—to print much and say nothing. 3. A literary laxative. 4. To put up money for a monkey monarchy.

MURDERER: 1. A savior of society. Synonyms: Soldier, hangman, doctor. 2. A man born ahead of or after his time.

MUSIC: 1. Anything that has charms to soothe a savage beast. 2. Unnecessary noises heard in restaurants and cheap hotels. 3. The only one of the arts that can not be prostituted to a base use. 4. An attempt to express the emotions that are beyond speech. 5. A noise less objectionable than any other noise.

MYSTIC: 1. One who guzzles his God. 2. A person who is puzzled before the obvious, but who understands the non-existent. 3. To stand over the vasty deep to summon monsters and slip in. 4. Sap that has lost its way. 5. A gymnast who turns flip-flops between the Here and the Not-Here. (Plato was the first mystic. It was he who announced the discovery of the Non-Existent. Hegel was the last mystic, for it was he who proved the Non-Existent was and was not, might have been and never could be, has was, is now, and never shall be.)

ATURE: 1. The Unseen Intelligence which loved us into being, and is disposing of us by the same token. 2. That which every one but a theologian understands, but which no one can define. 3. The Louvre of the Esthetic Eye; the abattoir of the Religious Eye; the charivari of the Ironic Eye. 4. The eternal Kishineff of an implacable God.

NANCY: A person of neither sex, who yet combines the bad qualities of both.

NIGGER: A colored person who has no money.

NEW THOUGHT: Plain, simple commonsense.

NEWSPAPER OFFICE: A figment factory.

NIETZSCHE (FRIEDRICH): A thunder smith.

NEBULOUS TYPOTHETÆ: A bum printer who can never be found when wanted.

NEIGHBOR: The man who knows more about you than you know about yourself.

NOTHING: 1. A negative which is the reality behind every ghostly affirmative. 2. Something that has density without weight, like a barber's breath.

NOMINATION: 1. Paradigrammatics, or the art of molding figures in plaster. 2. The call of the vile. 3. In democracies, the divine sacrament administered to ignorance. 3. The election, divination and apotheosis of a paramount parasite.

NEW YORK: The posthumous revenge of the Merchant of Venice.

NESBIT: A plenipotentiary of publicity who takes pretty nothings and makes of them New York Central literary hash.

BEDIENCE: 1. Expectation on a monument. 2. A dignified retreat from Balaklava. 3. Lex Talionis playing 'possum. 4. The second law of Nature, the first being murder. *E. g.*, "After all, it was my brother's Obedience to the Lord that laid the foundation of my glory."—From Cain's *Diary of an Altar-Wrecker.*

∞

OPPORTUNITY: 1. The only Knocker that is welcome. 2. Health and a job.

∞

OBLIVION: 1. The memory of Eternity. 2. A place where the human race and politicians are as one; where immortals are afflicted with aphasia; where God enjoys a long siesta; where we lose the bores and all those good folks who want to tell us the sad story of their lives.

∞

OLD MAID: A lady of uncertain age and uneasy virtue.

∞

OPERA: 1. Forerunner of the phonograph. 2. A rendezvous for the bored.

∞

OPTIMISM: 1. The instinct to lie. 2. Fatty degeneration of intelligence. 3. A philosophical system that attempts to demonstrate the existence of a pre-established Stupidity. 4. To believe that disease, dirt, earthquakes, fires, wars, politicians, blindness, and burial alive, celebrate and enhance the Glory of God. 5. To whistle while passing a cemetery in the night; to sing a hymn while having a tooth pulled; to smile while being robbed. 6. A tipple invented by Leigh Mitchell Hodges, the basis of which is clams and prune juice. 7. A kind of heart stimulant—the digitalis of failure.

∞

ORTHODOXY: 1. In religion, that state of mind which congratulates itself on being absolutely right, and a belief that all who think otherwise are wholly wrong. 2. A faith in the fixed—a worship of the static. 3. The joy that comes from thinking that most everybody is lined up for Limbus with no return ticket. 4. A condition brought about by the sprites of Humor, according to the rule that whom the gods would destroy they first make mad. 5. The zenith of selfishness and the nadir of egotism. 6. Mephisto with a lily in his hand. 7. A corpse that does not know it is dead. 8. Spiritual constipation. 9. That peculiar condition where the patient can neither eliminate an old idea or absorb a new one.

∞

ORGANIZED RELIGION: Antique philosophy, or the rule of the priest.

∞

OBSTINACY: 1. To stick to your favorite lie or truth because you know you are wrong in either case. 2. The ego's peacock-plumes.

∞

OPTIMIST: 1. A neurotic person with gooseflesh, and teeth a-chatter, trying hard to be brave. 2. A man who when he falls in the soup thinks of himself as being in the swim. 3. A man who does not care what happens, so long as it doesn't happen to him.

ORATORY: 1. Chin-music with Prince Albert accompaniment. 2. The lullaby of the Intellect. 3. Palaver in a Prince Albert.

ORIENT: 1. The subconscious part of the Occident. 2. The cradle of all infamies and all wisdom. 3. A place where God and the house have an esoteric meaning.

PAIN: 1. The sacred, immanent music of the Cosmos written in slow triple time. 2. A form of salvation invented by Christianity. 3. A beautiful and ecstatic state wherein one comes to a realization of the benevolence of the Almighty.

PARADISE: 1. A place where one is permitted to continue one's vices, excesses and inanities for an eternity. 2. A postmortem rake-off. 3. Any place from which one can see a friend in Hell. 4. One good telephone system. (Christians, Mohammedans and Billysundays have promised themselves a cheerful time after death; this they call *Paradise*. The Jews are the only people who have no Paradise beyond the tomb; this is easily explained when it is remembered that they own New York.)

PARODY: A calico cat stuffed with cotton.

PARVENU: One who has risen suddenly from nothing and becomes nothing suddenly.

PEACE: A monotonous interval between fights.

PEDANT: A person with more education than he can use.

PERFORMER: One who has a right to do troglodyte stunts and who can do something else.

PERFUME: Any smell that is used to down a worse one.

PHILOSOPHY: Our highest conception of life, its duties and its destinies.

POLITICIANS: 1. Men who volunteer the task of governing us for a consideration. 2. See Graftheimer.

PERICLES: See Aspasia.

PESSIMIST: 1. One who has been intimately acquainted with an Optimist. 2. The official vinegar-taster to Setebos.

PIETY: 1. The tinfoil of pretense. 2. That feeling of reverence we have toward the Almighty on account of His supposed resemblance to ourselves.

PUBLISHER: 1. An emunctory business, first functioned by Barabbas. 2. One of a band of panders which sprang into existence soon after the death of Gutenberg and which now overruns the world. 3. The patron saint of the mediocre.

POET: 1. A person born with the instinct to poverty. 2. One whose ideas of the beautiful and the sublime get him in jail or Potter's Field. 3. The patron saint of landlords. 4. A worthless, shiftless chap whose songs adorn the libraries of fat shopkeepers and paunchy Philistines one hundred years after the chap has died of malnutrition. 5. A dope-fiend.

POETRY: 1. A substitute for the impossible. 2. The bill and coo of sex.

∞

PLATONIC LOVE: The only kind that is blind. It never knows where it is going to fetch up.

∞

PLANET: A planet is a large body of matter entirely surrounded by a void, as distinguished from a clergyman, who is a large void entirely surrounded by matter.

∞

PLAY: A wise method of Nature which prevents one's nerves from setting on the outside of his Stein-Bloch.

∞

POCKET: The seat of the human soul.

∞

POLICE: Similia similibus.

∞

POLICY: Leaving a few things unsaid.

∞

POLITENESS: 1. The screen of language; the irony of civility; a fishing-rod. 2. A substitute for war. 3. To wipe your feet carefully on the common doormat before letting yourself in another's premises with a skeleton key. 4. Caliban in a boiled shirt, tuxedo and spats. (Politeness in the animal world is known after eating only; in the human world it is known both before and after eating, and, in a certain restricted circle, during eating.)

∞

PRAYER: A supplication intended for the person who prays. Only very dull people doubt its efficacy.

∞

PRIG: A person with more money than he needs.

∞

PREACHER: 1. Mendicancy in a celluloid collar. 2. A man who advises others concerning things about which he knows nothing. 3. Any man who lives on six hundred dollars a year and only works orally. 4. (Now obsolete) One who makes pastoral calls, frightens the young, astonishes the old, bothers the busy, and serves disappointed females as vicarious lover, father, friend, and personal representative of Deity.

∞

PRACTICAL POLITICS: The glad hand, and a swift kick in the pants.

∞

PRINCIPLE: 1. Bait. 2. A formula for doing a thing that, unformulated, would land the doer in jail. (Must not be confused with the word *principal*. Both words are used correctly in the following sentence: One may live one's life without principle, but not without principal. Or, again, Principle is sometimes principal; but principal has no principle. Or, The principal was never paid on principle.)

⊂⊃

PROSECUTOR: 1. One who abets a crime after it has or has not been committed. 2. An oratorical censor that precedes the coming of the hangman. 3. A pumice-stone that gives to the Statue of Justice a cleanly, Christian look. 4. A nose that can sniff the gallows, long before the wood is cut for it in the forest.

⊂⊃

POSTPONEMENT: The father of failure.

⊂⊃

PRISON: 1. A place where any lady may have a baby without fearing society. 2. An institution where even crooks go wrong. 3. The House of a Thousand Tears. 4. The last resort of the obscure to achieve fame. 5. A banker's mess-hall. 6. A place where men go to take the vow of chastity, poverty and obedience. 7. An example of a Socialist's Paradise, where equality prevails, everything is supplied, and competition is eliminated.

⊂⊃

PROTESTANTISM: 1. A splinter from the cross of Christ. 2. Acrobatic theologic mugwumpery. 3. Any one of fifty-seven varieties of hate. 4. Sects which have taken the petticoats off of the saints and put them on their pastors.

⊂⊃

PROGRESS: Getting free from theology, and substituting psychology instead.

⊂⊃

PROGRESSIVE: 1. A politician who wears his opinions pompadour. 2. An obstructionist who grows fat on conservatism and conversation. 3. A reactionary to whom movement and motion are necessary in order to keep warm, and secure gulps and guzzles. 4. A hungry or unsuccessful person; hence, an explosive, quixotic fellow with empty pockets and a shallow pate. 5. One who has felt the slings and arrows of outrageous success that has come to others. 6. A political piker, who will not play the game according to the rules which he himself devised. 7. One who would recall all decisions that do not uphold his claims. 8. A man who steals a label, and clapping it on himself, thinks that he is It. 9. A plan for going forward by backing up to mob rule. (The first Progressive of whom we know was Judas. The next was Ananias. Lazarus was a Progressive, and had he married the Queen of Sheba he would have changed places with Dives. *E. g.,* "This age belongs to the

Progressives."—From Kazook's *Confessions of a Popular Lick-Spittle*.)

PURGATORY: Two telephone systems in one town.

PROSPERITY: 1. That peculiar condition which excites the lively interest of the ambulance-chaser. 2. That which comes about when men believe in other men. 3. That condition which attracts the lively interest of lawyers, and warrants your being sued for damages or indicted, or both.

POLYGAMY: An endeavor to get more out of life than there is in it.

PSYCHOLOGY: The science of human minds and their relationship one to another.

PUBLIC OPINION: The judgment of the incapable many opposed to that of the discerning few.

PUNISHMENT: 1. The justice that the guilty deal out to those who are caught. 2. A perpetual fine, imposed hourly during the lifetime of a human being for his temerity in living, and continued in Heaven or Hell for his temerity in dying. 3. Among the poor and lowly, a service due the State for disobeying the mandates of the rich and powerful; among the rich, a slight reaction from overeating. (There are three kinds of punishment: the punishment of God, the punishment of man, and the punishment of living in Buffalo.)

POPULARITY: The triumph of the commonplace.

PROPHETS: The advance couriers of Time.

PURITY: 1. A rapt, interested and ecstatic aloofness toward natural processes. 2. A sewerage system that carries off everything, leaving the soul perfectly bald. 3. A condition of the mind that causes one to snoop around in garbage-dumps and start a league. 4. A plan of teaching things to children in which they are not interested. 5. An ethereal nose giving the miraculous power of sensing the lavatory in the Elysian Fields before it smells the flowers. (There is purity of mind, purity of body and purity of speech. Any one person endowed with all three of these modes or purity is blessed, elect, saved, or otherwise atrophied and pickled.)

PHARISEE: A man with more religion than he knows what to do with.

PHILISTINE: A term of reproach used by prigs to designate certain people they do not like.

PHILOSOPHER: One who thinks in order to believe; one who formulates his prejudices and systematizes his ignorance.

OYCROFT: 1. *Roy* means "king"; and *croft* means "home or craft." Thus, Roycroft means King-Craft; working for the highest; doing your work just as good as you can—making things for the King. 2. The dignity and the divinity of labor—peace, reciprocity, health, industry, persistency and endurance.

RELAXATION: The first requirement of strength.

RECIPROCITY: 1. The act of seconding the emotion. 2. A widow teaching a clergyman how to tango, in return for his kindness in having shown her how to swim.

RACE PROBLEM: Picking the winner.

RECIPE: 1. Work, smile, study, play, love—Mix. 2. Concentrate, Consecrate, Work.

REDEEMER: 1. A man who died that grafters might live. 2. An Oriental who would have forgiven Hiram Johnson. 3. The founder of a great trust, with headquarters in the Vatican. 4. Any one who consorts with the underworld, but who spends his vacation after death in the upper world. 5. In the Catholic Church the Man Higher Up, to whom the Pope plays Jack Rose. 6. One who saved the whole world, but who had himself damned for his pains. *E. g.*, First Citizen: "Christ was a myth." Second Citizen: "He was not!" (Then they murder each other in His Name.)

REASON: The arithmetic of the emotions.

RELIGION: Philosophy touched with emotion.

RAILROADS: The most important factor for progress and enlightenment in the world today.

RENUNCIATION: The act of giving up your seat in a street-car to a pretty woman, and then purposely stepping on an old man's toes.

REFORMER: 1. One who causes the rich to band themselves against the poor. 2. One who educates the people to appreciate the things they need.

REGION: A specific, definite space, as distinguished from any other specific, definite space; as, East Aurora, Barren Island, Kalamazoo, Sea Grit, Beverly.

REPARTEE: Any remark which is so clever that it makes the listener wish he had said it himself.

RESIGNATION: 1. A truce with ourselves in order to give us time to bury our living. 2. Pride walling itself up. 3. To keep shop without a show-window. 4. To go to sleep in the lap of the inevitable. 5. A covered walk to the interior of ourselves; a subway to some other form of trespass; a peephole into the enemy's fortress. 6. To play possum when one hears the footfall of Fate on the stairs.

REPUTATION: A bubble which a man bursts when he tries to blow it for himself.

RESURRECTION: The hypothetical New-Year's Day in the calendar of the dead.

REMORSE: That feeling which we all have when the thing fails to work, and the world knows it. The form that failure takes when it has made a grab and got nothing.

RESPECTABILITY: The dickey on the bosom of civilization.

ROMANCE: Where the hero begins by deceiving himself and ends by deceiving others.

RIGHTEOUS INDIGNATION: 1. Hate that scorches like hell, but which the possessor thinks proves he is right. 2. Your own wrath as opposed to the shocking bad temper of others.

RIGHTEOUSNESS: 1. Only a form of commonsense. 2. Wise expediency.

REVIVAL: Religion with a vaudeville attachment.

ROOSEVELT (THEODORE): A harangue-outang.

RUINS: 1. The hope of the ancient yesterday. 2. Absolute proof that the world of dreams, like the planet earth, is round. (Ruins are chiefly notable for the number of enlightened liars, called archeologists, they produce.)

ACRILEGE: 1. Any impolite act in the presence of a Humbug. 2. To shock the sensibilities of a Nobody. 3. To kill a mystical Mule or swap jokes in public with a Ghost.

SACRED SOIL: That which is well tilled.

SAINT: 1. Generally speaking, a person who retires into the wilderness of the spirit in order to coddle a ruling weakness. 2. To become polite toward God and His universe. 3. A steeplejack on miraged minarets.

SAINTSHIP: The exclusive possession of those who have either worn out or never had the capacity to sin.

SANITY: The ability to do team-work.

SALOON: The poor man's club; run with intent to make the poor man poorer.

SAVAGES: Men who like to go to war.

SANATORIUM: The place where a man is sent who has money, as opposed to "Bughouse," meaning the place where a man is sent who has no bank-balance.

SATIRIST: 1. A taxidermist of the Past, Present and Future; one who disembowels, stuffs and mounts all the gods, living and dead; one who fills up with straw and sawdust all illusions. 2. An esoteric mimic. 3. A being with an eye in the back of his head. 4. A postlude to the day's funeral march; a prelude to freedom.

SCANDAL: Gossip related by a small-bore.

SALVATION: Redemption from a belief in miracles.

SCHOLAR: 1. An ornate fossil. 2. A deadly ptomain that infests all forms of dynamic thought. 3. An impenetrable mass of matter that contains within itself the principle of unchangeability. 4. A turtle on whose shell is carved certain hieroglyphic lettering; such as, Ph. D., M. D., LL. D. 5. A medieval owl that roosts in universities, especially those that are endowed. 6. A plaster-of-Paris convolute. 7. A man, long on advice but short on action, who thinks he thinks. 8. One who draws his breath and salary. 9. Anybody with a bulging brow and no visible means of support.

SELF-RELIANCE: The name we give to the egotism of the man who succeeds.

SCHOOL: A training-place—mental, physical, moral. Good boys are boys at work. Bad boys are good boys who misdirect their energies.

SCIENCE: 1. The knowledge of the common people classified and carried one step further. 2. Accurate organized knowledge founded on fact. 3. Classified superstition.

SECRET: 1. A thing we give to others to keep for us. 2. Something known only to a few.

SEER: The scout of civilization.

SELF-CONTROL: The ability to restrain a laugh at the wrong place.

SILENCE: A trick of the human gullet that conceals weakness or emptiness.

SHEENY: A Jew who has more money than you have.

SHOAL: Shallow, literary, theological. (By extension, Columbia, Harvard, Yale and some other universities are sometimes called shoal-marks.)

SINCERITY: 1. A mental attitude acquired after long practise by man, in order to conceal his ulterior motives. 2. To be childish, to be senile. 3. To lack invention, imagination or character. (A sincere man is one who bluffs only a part of the time.)

SIN: Perverted power. The man without capacity for sin has no ability to do good—isn't that so? His soul is a Dead Sea that supports neither ameba nor fish, neither noxious bacilli nor useful life.

SERVILITY: 1. The instinct of superiority in its lowest form. 2. The politician's virtue. 3. A means of getting on. 4. A natural law, the violation of which makes one famous and poor.

SHERMAN ACT: A scheme to entrap men who set large numbers of people to work at employment profitable to everybody concerned.

SOBER: 1. To be bored, unhappy, "all in." 2. To be born or live in Philadelphia. 3. To be without money, to be destitute. 4. To die. *E. g.*, "Thank God, I am sober at last!" Dying words of Potodorus in *Two Gentlemen of Yonkers*.

SCOTCH: A verb meaning with care.

SELF-PROTECTION: The first law of life.

SOCIALIST: 1. A person easily peeved. 2. In economics, a school of thought founded by Cain. 3. A man who, so far as he himself is concerned, considers a thing done when he has suggested it.

∞

SMACK: A crude, rude, vulgar and unsatisfactory substitute for a kiss.

∞

SOCIETY: 1. An erotic clique that reads *Vogue, Smart Set* and *Town Topics.* 2. A congregation of people who are not persons. 3. A vast interchange of service through labor, ideas and commodities. 4. A relish for solitude.

∞

SOCIALISM: 1. A sincere, sentimental, beneficent theory, which has but one objection, and that is, it will not work. 2. A plan by which the inefficient, irresponsible, ineffective, unemployable and unworthy will thrive without industry, persistence or economy. 3. An earnest effort to get Nature to change the rules for the benefit of those who are tired of the Game. 4. A social and economic scheme of government by which man shall loiter rather than labor. 5. A survival of the unfit. 6. A device for swimming without going near the H_2O.. 7. Participation in profits without responsibility as to deficits. 8. An arrangement for destroying initiative, invention, creation and originality. 9. Resolutions passed by a committee as a substitute for work. 10. A sentiment which encouraged and evolved would lead to revolution, with dynamiting and destruction as a prominent and recognized part of its propaganda. 11. A system for turning water into wine, kerosene into oyster-soup, and boulders into bread, by passing resolutions.

∞

SOCIOLOGY: The religious application of economics.

∞

SORROW: The magical palette upon which Life mixes her colors.

∞

SLAVE: A person with a servile mind, who quickly crooks the pregnant hinges of the knee, that thrift may follow fawning; who gratifies his wants either through cringing flattery or coercion, and who tyrannizes over others whenever he has a chance.

∞

SPECIALIST: 1. One who limits himself to his chosen mode of ignorance, and gets further into a bog than the man ahead of him. 2. A kind of hypnotic trance wherein a person by centering his gaze on a given object renders the object smaller in proportion as his illusion grows.

∞

SOREHEAD: A politician who has reached for something that was not his, and missed.

SOLITUDE: The only thing that can hold the balance true.

SORCERER: 1. Any one who can make the people of the United States believe they rule. 2. A juggler (hence the founder of any religious, political or philosophical system).

SPECIOUS: That form of argument used as an indoor sport by East Aurora natives in an attempt to prove that two or three make four.

SORCERY: The art of charming money out of the pockets of those who do not desire to part with it.

SPINSTERHOOD: An achievement, not a disgrace.

STALL STUFF: 1. Things said to see what the other person will say. 2. The language used by politicians. 3. All conversation between spoons. *Example*: Seeing Mr. Jones leave his office, you enter and ask his stenographer this question: "Is Mr. Jones in?" (See Piffle, Pink Tea, Four o'Clock.)

STAR: 1. A milestone in the Infinite. 2. A malicious, ironic eye. 3. A device to show man his insignificance.

STARVATION: 1. The originator of thought. 2. A way to salvation. 3. A physical eccentricity of the stomach. 4. A cure for indigestion. 5. A banting process invented by Lazarus.

SPECIALIZATION: The ability to focus all your energies on one thing.

STUDIO: 1. A place where a model is borne to blush unseen, and contract pneumonia in the chilly air. 2. A rendezvous of would-bes, has-beens and never-wazzers. 3. A place to study the esoteric. 4. The most polite term you can apply to it.

STUPIDITY: 1. The Utopia of the wise, the Lethe forbidden to the lips of genius. 2. The driving power of a Mass in motion. 3. An incurable state of somnambulism with which mankind is blessed, and under the spell of which it performs the most fantastic actions, such as marriage, balloting, warring, preaching, selling, buying, baptizing. 4. The *leit-motif* of the Vaudeville called Progressiveness.

∝⊃

SUPERSTITION: 1. Scrambled science flavored with fear. 2. Ossified metaphor.

∝⊃

SURGERY: An adjunct, more or less valuable to the diagnostician.

∝⊃

STYLE: 1. The brogue of the mind. 2. A certain manner or deportment which emanates from those who have neither manner nor deportment. 3. A peculiar and individual manner of doing the unnecessary.

∝⊃

SUBSIDIARY: A competitor who has come off his perch through threats or bribes, or both.

∝⊃

SUCCESS: 1. A sunset by Turner. 2. A stained-glass window through which one may see an ironic moon. 3. The final link in a chain of chalk. 4. To rise from the illusion of pursuit to the disillusion of possession. 5. An inability to further fletcherize. 6. Giving up the fight, being possessed of the fallacy that you have won. 7. Death's lullaby. 8. The accomplishment of one's best. 9. To write your name high upon the outhouse of a country tavern. 10. A constant sense of discontent, broken by brief periods of satisfaction on doing some specially good piece of work. 11. A matter of outliving your sins. 12. A subtle connivance of Nature for bringing about a man's defeat. 13. The realization of the estimate which you place upon yourself. 14. Voltage under control— keeping one hand on the transformer of your Kosmic Kilowatts. 15. A matter of the red corpuscle. 16. The thing that spoils many a good failure. 17. Something that is hideous to all but its victims.

∝⊃

SUCTION: An automatic, murderous and perpetual movement of Society against each individual.

∝⊃

SUPERNATURAL: The natural not yet understood.

∝⊃

SUN: 1. A giant spot-light, which from the wings of space plays intermittently upon a meaningless ten-twenty-thirty vaudeville show. 2. The root of all evil, the mother of all beauty, and the final tomb of all that is good, bad or indifferent. 3. A dyehouse, probably the first. (The sun was once worshiped as a divinity, but later the competition between gods and divinities became so strenuous that the sun was forgotten, hence his casual earthquakes, floods and other little reminders that we and our gods are only his gimcracks.)

STATUTE: The proof, record and final justification of the infallibility of Ignorance.

STRONG MAN: One who busies himself with the useful tasks that others can not, or will not do, and allows those who can do nothing else to do the easy things.

SYMPATHY: 1. A malady that sometimes afflicts the rich. 2. The lees of the wine-cup offered to another. 3. An impulse toward ourselves through the heart of another. 4. Whatever may be extended to another that does not take the shape of money. 5. The sum of all virtues. 6. The first attribute of love as well as its last. (I am not sure but that sympathy is love's own self, vitalized mayhap by some divine actinic ray. Only the souls who have suffered are well loved.)

EACHER: 1. A person, either male or female, who instils into the head of another person, either voluntarily or for pay, the sum and substance of his or her ignorance. 2. One who makes two ideas grow where only one grew before.

TALK: To open and close the mouth rapidly while the bellows in the throat pumps out the gas in the brain.

TAFTIAN: Any man who is too cowardly to fight, and too fat to run.

TEMPTATION: A desire to do something you know you should not do.

THEOLOGICAL SEMINARY: A place where young men are taught to silence the questions of the ignorant.

TEMPLE: A place other than a bed, where one takes one's shoes off. (There are Jewish temples, pagan temples and money temples, but no Christian temples: the latter has no need of them, because Christian religion is the only one in the world in which its believers and followers practise exactly what its Founder taught. Each Christian may point to himself and say proudly, "Ecce Temple," hence, etc., etc., etc.)

THE PHILISTINE: A publication that puts the Syracuse Product on the terminal feathers of the Idea Bird.

THE-SCENE-CHANGES: A device invented by a writer who was running short of Cosmic Gasoline.

TOMORROW: The mother of regret.

THANKSGIVING: 1. A mass said for the repose of the living. 2. Gratitude in the presence of the death of some one else. 3. The irony of fatality. 4. The instinctive and perpetual atavism of the Will-to-Live. (Thanksgiving-Day in the United States is a national holiday on which all the people who during the past year have survived earthquake, fire, housemaid's knee and death, overeat and thus thank God for His favoritism.)

TIGHTWADITY: A disease in which one dollar obstructs the vision to the exclusion of a higher denomination.

TOLERANCE: An agreement to tolerate intolerance.

TODAY: The hearse that carries the dreams of yesterday to the cemetery.

THE: An article, aristocratic by birth and breeding, but which degenerates into an adjective in the sentence, "He is THE man of the hour."

THEOLOGY: 1. A hideous juggernaut to whose wheels cling the blood and bone and the flattened flesh of a million dead emotions. 2. Not what we know about God, but what we do not know about Nature. 3. Obsolete psychology, or the arbitrary rule of a Theos or god. 4. An engine planned for the purpose of bewildering humanity. 5. Self-deceived egotism, hiding behind the name of Deity. 6. Antique and obsolete philosophy. 7. The science of a non-existent, all-powerful, all-wise and all-loving nix.

THINKER: 1. One who destroys philosophies. 2. One who can make others think.

THOUGHT: 1. Something made up of the thoughts you, yourself, think. The other kind is supplied to you by jobbers. 2. Mental dynamite.

TIME: 1. The press-agent of genius. 2. An eternal guest that banquets on our ideals and bodies. 3. In the theater of the gods a moving-picture film that reproduces the cosmic comedy. 4. A metaphysical entity that made the Ingersoll watch a physical possibility. 5. A loafer playing at tenpins. 6. An illusion—to orators. 7. The solvent and the dissolver of all. (Time was anciently symbolized by Kronos; today it is symbolized by the mystical syllables, So-Much-Per. The word has also undergone strange etymological changes. Anciently, time was singular, but since the advent of the Unions, we have "time and a third," "double time," etc.)

TOMB: A place for the deposit of the dead. (See College, Newspaper Office, Philadelphia Club, Legation, etc.)

TOP-NOTCHER: An individual who works only for the interest of the institution of which he is a part, not against it.

TOTAL DEPRAVITY: The greatest idea for the acquisition of power and pelf ever devised.

TROUBLE: 1. A hallucination that affords a sweet satisfaction to the possessor. 2. Any interesting topic of conversation. 3. A plan of Nature whereby a person is diverted from the humiliation of seeing himself as others see him. (An impressario's troubles begin when the prima donna kicks and the ladies of the ballet won't.)

TRUMPET: A musical instrument which in the mouth of Gabriel will bring to life for their eternal undoing all Shylocks, officeholders, editorial writers, landlords, and professional epigrammatists.

TITLE: 1. A Pantheon of royal ciphers. 2. Anything superimposed on a superfluity.

TRUTH: 1. A universal error. 2. A relation between one illusion (the outer world) and another (the inner world). 3. A prejudice raised to an axiom. 4. Something that a few will die for. 5. That which serves us best in expressing our lives. (A rotting log is truth to a bed of violets; while sand is truth to a cactus.) 6. Anything which happened, might have happened, or which will possibly happen. 7. The opinion that still survives. 8. An imaginary line dividing error into two parts.

TRADITION: 1. Salvation through ossification; redemption through folklore; a fetter for the foolish. 2. A clock that tells what time it was. 3. A method of holding the many back while some man does the thing which they declare is impossible.

NIVERSITY: 1. An institution for the prevention of learning. 2. A place where rich men send their sons who have no aptitude for business. 3. A plan for the elimination of physical culture and the exaltation of athletics. 4. A literary, gonococci culture-bed. 5. A collection of buildings which emit the odor of the classics and omit the odor of sanctity. 6. A place wherein the youthful mind is taught the danger of thinking.

Union Labor: A force which unchecked would develop into violent and destructive anarchy.

United States of America: Miss District de Columbia and her forty-eight Subsidiaries.

Unrequited: (Used generally with the word love.) Inability to make both ends meet.

Utopian: A person who demands that you shall live up to his ideals.

Unpardonable Sin: Neglecting to close the screen-door.

Up to Date: To be far behind the Ancients, who were generally ahead of the current date. *E. g.*, "This thing would never have happened if I had only been up to date, but I tried to be dateless."—Last words of Socrates.

Utopia: A place where you have but to suggest a thing, to consider it done; a condition where all things are supplied on slipping a wish into a slot.

Usage: The consecration in time of something that was originally absurd.

ICIOUS: 1. To be natural. 2. To give up lying. (A word taken from the Zynrxi, and first used by the French at the Siege of Paris to describe the Germans; hence, any one who does anything impolite or acts in any way strictly in accordance with his innate tastes.)

VENOM: 1. The juice of hate. 2. The sap of reformers, moralists and socialists. 3. The deadly smile of the optimist when he looks at the under dog. 4. The physical sweat of a defeated candidate and the emotional sweat of old maids. (Venom, like everything else, is subject to the law of evolution and variation. Between the venom of Cain and the venom of Tolstoy, several million instances could be quoted to prove the universality and beneficence of this breedy instinct.)

VICTORY: A matter of staying-power.

VACILLATION: The prominent feature of weakness of character.

VAUDEVILLE: A matter of verve, nerve and vermilion.

VERACITY: The appendix vermiformis of the human character; a quaint atavistic instinct. (Veracity was once quite common in the childhood of the race; but as herding became more and more complex and human relations became more and more interjangled, there came into being a species of bipeds known as doctors, lawyers, politicians, editorial writers and preachers. Coeval with their birth the instinct to veracity weakened perceptibly until it reached the condition of nixus nihilus ni in which we hold it today.)

VACATION: A period of increased and pleasurable activity when your wife is at the seashore.

VIVISECTION: Blood-lust, screened behind the sacred name of Science.

VILE: 1. Anything that serves; whatever is useful. 2. Something done or thought by some one else.

VINDICATION: The subtlest form of irony.

ADSWORTH: 1. A fabled people, whose remains are found in the Genesee Valley, who chased an anise-seed bag around the steamheat and pretended to be bored by existence. 2. Any one with more buzz-fuzz than brains.

WARRIOR: 1. A soldier de luxe. 2. A successful, patriotic thug who has been dead fifty years or more. 3. A fearless person who gains renown by the number of alcoholic drinks he has taken in a day and by the variety and virulence of the venereal diseases he has contracted. 4. A myth, a fable, a lie.

WAVES: The thoughts of the sea, which, like human wave-thoughts, roll on, roll back, roll up and spray the void.

WEALTH: A cunning device of Fate whereby men are made captive, and burdened with responsibilities from which only Death can file their fetters.

WIFE: 1. In good society, a publicity agent who advertises her husband's financial status through conspicuous waste and conspicuous leisure. 2. In the submerged tenth, a punching-bag and something handy for batting up flies. 3. A man's mental mate, and therefore his competitor in the race for power. 4. The other half of the sphere. (This view is usually regarded as a vagary, and any one holding it is apt to be pointed out as strange, peculiar, erratic and unsafe.)

WINE: An infallible antidote to commonsense and seriousness; an excuse for deeds otherwise unforgivable.

WISDOM: A term Pride uses when talking of Necessity.

WISE MAN: One who sees the storm coming before the clouds appear.

Wit: The thing that fractures many a friendship.

Woman: 1. The First Cause. 2. A being created for the purpose of voting. 3. Any one with an allowance that is occasionally paid, but which can't be collected. 4. A pet, a plaything, a scullion, a thing to die for, or a thing to kill. 5. A being to get rid of or to secure—to run away from, or with, as the case may be. 6. Among the Ancients, a slave, a chattel; among the Moderns, a financial swashbuckler. Synonyms: sphinx, devil, angel, liar, spendthrift.

War: The sure result of the existence of armed men.

We: The smear of life against the radiant x.

Whisky: The Devil's right bower.

Words: The airy, fairy humming-birds of the imagination.

Wordsworth (William): The only Lilliputian that slipped under the canvas into Olympus.

Work: 1. That which keeps us out of trouble. 2. A plan of God to circumvent the Devil.

Worms: 1. The final word in criticism. 2. At the last analysis.

Worry: Ironic nurse to old bedridden Dame Care. *E. g.*, "I should worry"— famous saying of the Infinite Nix at twelve o'clock Saturday night of the Sixth Day as he threw down his tools and sent the Earth about its business.

ESTERDAY: 1. One evil less and one memory more. 2. A short-change artist, from whom we can never recover. 3. A period of time that has always existed, in contradistinction to a period of time called tomorrow that can never exist. 4. A mirror wherein if we look long enough we will see ourselves as others could never possibly see us. 5. The Eden of the sentimental. (Time is divided into yesterday, today and tomorrow, which are but three varieties of the same metaphysical tetter. In the beginning was the Infinite, and the Infinite begat Time, and Time begat Yesterday, Today and Tomorrow.)

YOUR DUTY: The things you have to do, and not a damn tap more. The other man's duty is the thing you think he should do.

YOURS: Anything which up to the present time the bunch has not been able to get

away from you.

ODIAC: 1. The wallpaper of the heavens. 2. The mirrors of the nothingness of Man and the sublimity of the nothingness of Space.

ZEAL: The feeling you have before you secure the thing, as compared with "Stung," which is your condition after you have captured it.

ZONE: The region immediately surrounding a Limburger Cheese.

ZERO: A round figure often referred to by Doctor Cook in his diary, and which his enemies tried to make symbolic of himself.

ZIGZAG: The route followed by poets in arriving at truth, as opposed to the direct course which they take for the buffet.

ZEUS: A grouchy old god who was so reduced in estate that he posed as a model for Greek artists.

ZEPHYR: A ladylike blizzard.

ZEITGEIST: The things that everybody believes, but that nobody understands.